Three Brilliant Stories!

The Big Fight
The Lucky Stone
The Longship

Find out more about Shoo Rayner and Viking Vik at www.shoorayner.com

Published by Shoo Rayner

www.shoorayner.com

ISBN 978 1 908944 33 7

First published in Great Britain in 2008

First paperback publication in 2009

by ORCHARD BOOKS

This edition 2017

A CIP catalogue record for this book is available from the British Library.

For Clara and Esme

Viking Vik

and the Big Fight

"I'm the leader!" Vik yelled, thrusting his wooden sword towards the sky.

"No, you're not!" Wulf snarled. "I'm the leader!"

Wulf bounded up the sharp ridge of the Dragon rock. The two boys stared into each other's eyes.

There was no great love between them. Wulf pulled a wooden club from his belt and swung at Vik.

Vik ducked, swung his sword and caught Wulf a glancing blow on the arm.

"Ow! Now you've done it," Wulf hissed. "I'll show you who's the leader."

Wulf leapt on top of Vik. The two boys grappled and slid down the side of the rock into the gritty dust below.

They punched, they bit, they pinched and they kicked.

Vik's dog Fleck, yapped and barked and tried to help his master.

10

The Dragon Rock

The Dragon Rock, on the beach at Snekkevik, is really two rocks that look like the head and body of a dragon that is half buried in the sand. Children have always met and played on the Dragon Rock. They pretend they're flying on the dragon's back, or they just play "King of the Castle".

"Stop!" Shouted Freya. "Why do you two always have to fight?" She grabbed her brothers and tried to pull them apart. "For Odin's sake, will you please stop it!"

Wulf lashed out, hoping to silence Vik for good.

"Waaaah!"

Freya's piercing scream stopped both boys in their tracks. Freya's hands were pressed to her mouth. She glared at Wulf. Tears fell from her eyes, which flashed with the anger that burned inside her.

"Err… I'm sorry, Freya," Wulf began. "I didn't think, I just…"

Freya pulled her hands away from her mouth. Blood trickled from her bottom lip.

"You never think!" She snapped back at him.

The two boys hung their heads in shame.

"Are you all right, Freya?" Vik asked.

Freya explored her swollen lip with
her tongue and checked that she still
had all her teeth.

"I suppose so," she mumbled.

But Freya was angry.
She put her hands on her hips and
told the two boys exactly what she
thought of them.

"You're pathetic! You're always fighting to be the leader. Well, it takes more than strength to be the leader. It takes courage and brains, too."

"You should have a competition to decide who is the leader once and for all."

"Hey! That's a really good idea," said Wulf.

"But what sort of competition did you have in mind?" Vik asked, cautiously.

"Hmmm... I'll think of something," Said Freya.

Competitions

Vikings love having
competitions to decide who is…

… the fiercest

… the strongest

… the greediest   … and the meanest

"How about a running race?" Vik suggested.

"No… you're easily the fastest," Freya replied. "That would be unfair."

"Err...how about a swimming race?" said Wulf.

"No! You've got such big feet, you swim like a dolphin," Freya laughed. "That would be unfair, too."

Suddenly Freya clapped her hands. "I know! You shall have an eating competition."

"Mmmm!" The boys rubbed their stomachs. "That sounds good," they chimed together.

"Okay, that's what we'll do." Freya smiled secretly to herself. "I'll make the rules, and I'll choose what you eat."

The boys weren't sure, but they couldn't say no to Freya, not while her lip was still swollen and lumpy.

"I'll go and get everything ready. Meet back here later, and no fighting!" Freya ordered.

It was late in the
afternoon before
Freya was ready.
She placed six bowls,
in two rows of three,
on the Dragon rock.

The bowls had
lids so the boys
couldn't see what
was inside. Fleck
sniffed them with
great interest.

"Now… you have to swallow a whole mouthful and show me your empty mouth," Freya explained. "If you're sick afterwards, that's okay."

"Sick?!" Wulf yelped. "Why… what do you want us to eat?"

Freya handed them a bowl each and, with a flourish, she whisked the lids off and announced, "Eel jelly!"

Disgusting things to eat

Vikings don't have freezers, so most of the food in their larders is a little bit mouldy. You might find…

Mouldy sheep's heads

Old, sour, mouldy goat's milk

Soft, mouldy goose fat

Hard, dried, mouldy bread

"Urrrrgh!" The boys stared at
the cold, shimmering, green-grey,
wobbling mess in their bowls.
Fleck look disgusted. He ran away to
find something nice to eat.

"Do we have to?" Wulf whined.

Vik looked at Freya's lip. This wasn't just about who became the leader – the honour of both boys was at stake.

Vik took a
handful of jelly
and put it in his
mouth. It was the
most revolting
thing he had ever
tasted. He tried to
swallow, but his
stomach wouldn't
let him.
Vik closed his
eyes and relaxed.
The jelly slid
down his throat as
if it were live eels
wriggling their
way down the
river.

30

Vik opened his empty mouth and
Freya clapped her hands.

"Well
done!" she
said, as Vik
shuddered
violently.

As Vik lay on the ground retching, Wulf cleared his throat.

"Mmmm! That was delicious!"

He threw his head back and showed Freya his empty mouth and clean bowl.

"Your stomach must be made of iron," Freya said, suspiciously.

Freya handed out the bowls for the next challenge. "Try eating these..."

"Worms!" Vik felt sick already. "We don't have to eat them all do we?"

"No. You only have to eat one," Freya explained, smiling sweetly, if a little bit lopsidedly..

Wulf was winning.
Vik knew he needed to be
really brave. He chose the
cleanest worm, closed his
eyes and put it in his mouth.

"You don't have
to chew it,"
Freya said,
sweetly.

This time Vik really could feel the worm wriggling in his throat as it slithered into his stomach.

He showed Freya his empty mouth, then he fell to the ground choking and gagging.

"Mmmmm! That was delicious!" Wulf boasted. "What's for pudding?" He had emptied his bowl once again!

Like a magician performing a trick Freya lifted the lids of their last bowls.

Vik's stomach churned. Shiny balls of frogspawn, like a hundred tiny eyeballs, stared coldly at him from his bowl.

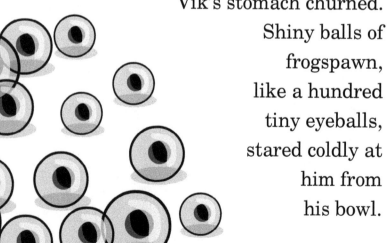

38

He couldn't let Wulf win. He scooped up a handful and put them in his mouth.

He shook his head and fought the revolting, slimy, sloppy balls down into his stomach.

Freya clapped her hands. "Well done, Vik! You can be sick now!"

"Mmmm!" that was delicious!" Wulf threw his empty bowl on the floor and leapt onto the Dragon Rock. "I ate more than Vik and I wasn't sick, either. That makes me the winner!"

Vik lay in the dirt. His stomach
ached and his throat burned.
A revolting taste lingered in his
mouth. He fought to keep the tears
away. It was so unfair. He had eaten
everything but he'd still lost.

Through his tears, he saw Wulf
march up and down the Dragon Rock,
preening himself like a peacock, a
smug grin was plastered all over
his face. But there was something
about Wulf's stomach… it moved in
a mysterious, gloopy way. Then Vik
remembered a story about Thor,
who tricked a dragon in an
eating contest

Had Wulf done
the same – had
he tricked Vik
and Freya?

The story of
Thor and the Dragon.

The great god, Thor, had an eating competition with a dragon. Beforehand, Thor filled a leather bag with porridge and hid it under his jerkin. When he had eaten his fill, he took a knife and cut the bag open. The porridge seemed to ooze out of his stomach!

"I'm making room for more food," he said.

When the dragon realised that Thor could empty his stomach whenever he wanted, it gave up and let Thor win the competition.

"You cheat!"
Vik snarled.

Wulf stared
blankly as Vik
scrambled up
the rock and
flew at him.
Vik grappled
with Wulf's belt
and pulled until
the buckle broke.
There was a
horrible, squidgy,
slurping noise,
then Wulf groaned
as eel jelly, worms
and frogspawn slid
slowly down the
top of his
trousers.

Wulf had poured the disgusting food down his leather jerkin while Freya was watching Vik being sick. He had remembered the story of Thor and the dragon, too.

Now the revolting mess slipped down the inside of his trouser legs and into his boots.

Holding himself as if he'd wet his pants, Wulf skulked back to the village to clean himself up.

"You were so brave, eating all that revolting stuff," Freya told Vik. "I didn't think you'd really do it, you know?"

"I had to," Vik explained. "After Wulf hit you, it was the only way to regain our honour. And Wulf still cheated!"

Vik watched the pathetic figure of Wulf as he tiptoed his way back home.

47

Vik stood tall on the Dragon rock. "You'll never be the leader!" He called after Wulf. "Because you haven't got the guts!"

The End

and the Lucky Stone

"There's loads of driftwood on the beach," said Vik.

"I'm not going all the way down there," Wulf grumbled.

"C-c-can't we find some wood up here?" Freya shivered. "It's too cold to go climbing down those rocks."

Mum had told the children to find some kindling wood for the fire. Winter was drawing in. The dark sky forecast snow, they needed all the wood they could get.

"Well, I'm going down there… come on, Fleck!" Vik and his faithful dog scrambled down the rocks to the beach.

Freya called
after them.
"We'll go and
look for wood
in the forest
over there."

In no time at all, Vik had collected lots of sticks, which he tied into bundles with long strips of leather.

"Come on, Fleck. It's started snowing... let's go!" Vik looked all around him, but Fleck had disappeared.

Vik ran down the beach calling Fleck's name, but he was nowhere to be seen.

Vik wasn't worried, Fleck ran off all the time. He must've found something tasty to chase, Vik thought to himself.

"I'm going home, Fleck," Vik yelled. "I'm not waiting!"

As he turned to go, Vik spotted something on the ground. A smooth white stone stood out against the gritty, grey sand. It had shining green and brown stripes on it"s surface. A perfect hole has been worn through at one end – almost as if it had been made by a jeweller.

Vik tied a leather strip through the hole and hung it around his neck. "It's my lucky stone," he told himself.

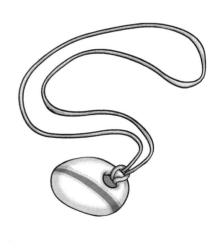

Just then, with
a joyous bark,
Fleck appeared
from behind
some rocks.
He leapt in the
air, trying to
catch the huge
snowflakes that
were now falling
thick and fast.

Viking Weather

Vikings live in the far, far north. When it snows it really, really snows!

The snow can stay on the ground all winter.

Vikings use skis and sleighs to get about on the snow.

Vik picked up his
snow-covered bundles
and scrambled over
the rocks. The wind
blew large white
flakes into his
eyes.

The ground was already hidden
under a layer of fluffy snow.
Everything looked different.
Vik headed towards the forest.

"Wulf! Freya! Where are you?"

The snow made everything quiet and dampened the sound of his voice. All he could hear was the tramp of his feet and the wind blowing through the trees.

It was late, the sky was dark and
the snow was falling heavily.
Vik felt very small and very alone.
The path was covered by the
snow and Vik had lost all
sense of direction.

"Which way, Fleck?"

Fleck stared at him. His look
seemed to say, "I don't know.
You're the leader!"

"The sun sets in the west,"
Vik explained. "If we head
towards the darkest bit of sky,
we should get home quite soon.
Come on!" Vik didn't believe it,
but it made him feel better.

Fleck followed.
His master was
always right,
wasn't he?

67

It was really dark now, and the snow was very deep. Vik was well and truly lost. He pulled his cloak around himself and shivered. "We're going to die," he told Fleck. "They'll find us frozen into blocks of ice."

"Woof!"
Fleck barked and
ran ahead. Vik
strained his eyes.
Was that a light?

As Vik struggled
through the snow, the
light grew brighter.
"Well done, Fleck!" he
said excitedly.
"It's a house!"

How not to get lost in The Forest

If you are lost in a Viking Forest, look at the tree trunks for a natural compass. Moss and lichen like the shade, so they grow best on the north side of the trunks. Now you can work out south, east and west!

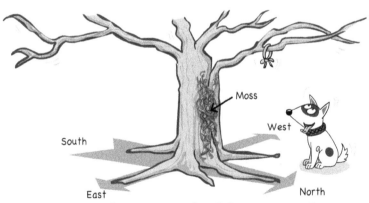

You can also tie red ribbons on the branches to mark your way back home.

The door opened
a crack. All Vik
could see was a
pair of suspicious
eyes. A thin, reedy
voice spoke:
"Who's there?"

"My name is Vik Haraldson."
Vik's teeth chattered. "I'm lost
and I'm f-f-freezing to d-d-death!"

The door opened a little more.
An old, bent woman looked Vik up
and down.

"I can't leave you out there to freeze, but I don't want any funny business. I've got absolutely no food in the house, so don't expect me to feed you," she said.

Vik was so pleased to be let into the warm, he didn't care about food.

But once Vik could feel his toes again, his stomach began to rumble, and soon food was all he could think about!

Vik sat by the little fire. He played with his lucky stone and wondered what the great god, Thor would do...

Thor and his Goats

Thor's chariot is pulled by two goats. When Thor is hungry, he cooks the goats and eats them.

If Thor wraps the bones up in the skins, he can bring the goats back to life. Now that really is fast food!

A cunning plan popped into Vik's head. He winked at Fleck before he said, "We could eat my dog!"

"Your dog?" The woman said, startled. Fleck tucked his tail between his legs and whimpered.

"Yes," Vik sighed. "Of course, we'd have to use my lucky stone. Dog doesn't taste very nice on its own."

The old woman eyed Vik suspiciously. "How does that work, then?" She asked.

"We need to boil a large pot of water," Vik explained. "We can use the wood I brought to build a fire."

The woman became quite excited and helped Vik get everything ready.

When the water was boiling, they dropped his lucky stone into the pot.

Then he tested it with a spoon.

"Mmmm! Not bad," He
declared. "But it would
taste so much better
with an onion."

"Let me see what I've got," said the old woman. She shuffled off and returned with a large onion - even though she had absolutely no food in the house!

When it had been sliced and added to the water, Vik tasted it again.

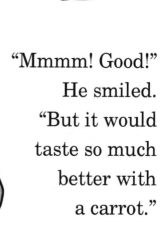

"Mmmm! Good!" He smiled. "But it would taste so much better with a carrot."

82

The woman tasted it and agreed. "Let me see what I've got," she said.

Soon, she came back with a large carrot - even though she had absolutely no food in the house!

"Yum!" said Vik. "It's really beginning to taste like something now. But it would be so much better with a handful of beans."

83

And so the evening went on. Every time Vik tasted the soup, he suggested another ingredient, and the old woman always managed to find what he asked for - even though she had absolutely no food in the house! She even found some salt and pepper.

Soon the lucky stone had magically turn the water into a delicious soup.

Soup Recipe

Get a grown-up Viking to help you fry some sliced onions in a casserole dish, until they are soft and brown.

Add some water or vegetable stock and some chopped vegetables, beans, salt and pepper, and maybe some herbs.

Cook long and slow on a low heat.

Don't forget to add your lucky stone for that extra, wonderful flavour. You had better give it a good wash first!

"Now for the dog!" said Vik, picking up a huge knife.

"Oh!" said the old woman, who by now had become quite fond of Fleck.

"Of course, dog meat *is* pretty disgusting," Vik said, "even with a lucky stone. If only we had some other meat."

The old woman looked at
Fleck. Fleck stared back
at her with his big, brown,
trusting eyes.

"Let me
see what
I've got,"
she said.

The woman found some cold, cooked-meat and a loaf of bread too - even though she had absolutely no food in the house! Soon they filled themselves up with the best meal either could remember, and Fleck busied himself chewing the bone.

"That was wonderful," the old woman said. "And to think it was all made with your lucky stone!"

Vik smiled, snuggled down in front of the fire with Fleck and fell into a deep and happy sleep.

They woke the next day to the sound of voices shouting Vik's name. The snow had settled and the sky was clear and blue. Freya and Wulf were searching for him.

"Vik!" Freya laughed when she saw him. "We were worried that you'd frozen to death!"

Vik hugged his sister. "This kind lady took us in."

91

"He's a wonderful cook," the old woman said. "He can make a meal out of nothing." Then she explained how Vik had made the tastiest meal, even though she had absolutely no food in the house!

As Vik turned to go back home with Freya and Wulf, the old woman held up Vik's lucky stone. It had turned a brown, soupy colour, and didn't shine like it had before.

"You keep it," said Vik. "It's a present to say thank you for saving me last night."

"Thank you!" The old woman exclaimed. "Now I shall never go hungry. Do drop by if you're ever passing . Now I can always make some lucky stone soup."

"Thanks!" smiled Vik. "Come on, Fleck... let's go!"

The End

and the Longship

The dragon glowered as Vik, Freya and Wulf stood hypnotised by it's hard, staring eyes.

"She's beautiful," said Vik, running his hand down the dragon's long neck. "I wish we could sail in her."

"Me too," Wulf and Freya echoed.

Just then, Jarl Magnusson came striding down the jetty. "A Longship is no place for children," he boomed.

"Oh, Dad!" Freya fluttered her eyelashes. She knew how to get around her father – but it didn't work this time.

"Longships are definitely not for girls!" He told her firmly.

Vik yearned to sail on a Longship. Just like his father, the sea flowed in Vik's blood. "Will we ever get to sail in her?" He sighed.

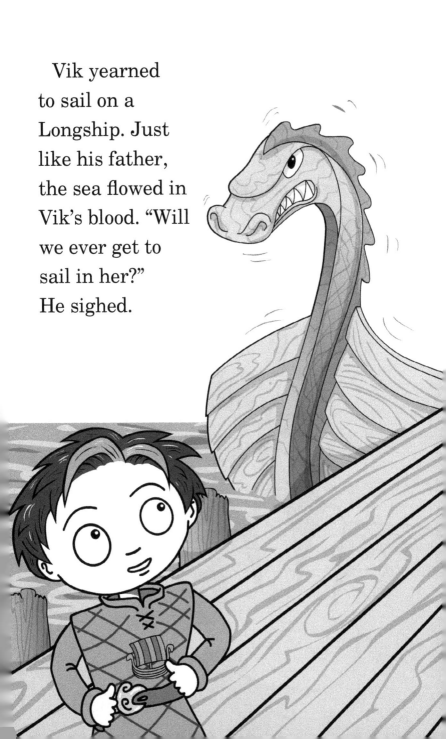

Jarl Magnusson smiled, and spoke gently to Vik. "When you are strong enough and old enough to understand the dangerous ways of the ocean, then you can sail on board a Longship."

Jarl Magnusson turned to his men and began shouting orders. "Come on, you slack-jawed jellyfish! Get this ship ready before the weather changes. It's time to put the *Dragon* through her paces."

The *Dragon* was brand-new. For the last few months, Vik had watched her being built on the shore at Snekkevik. The graceful ship had not yet been out of their little fiord. It was time she was tested on the high seas.

Fiords

During the ice ages, glaciers cut deep valleys into the rocky mountains in Scandinavia.

When the glaciers melted, the valleys were flooded by the sea and became fiords.

Fiords are very deep and give excellent shelter for ocean-going ships.

"We can watch her sail from the skerries," Vik suggested.

"Good idea," said Wulf. "Let's go."

The three children and Vik's dog, Fleck, ran all the way to the mouth of the fiord.

The skerries were a chain of small islands that reached out into the sea like a rocky necklace.

Flek splashed in the rock pools.
It was low tide and the children soon
hopped out to the furthest island,
where they waited for the *Dragon* to
sail past.

"We're quite f-f-far out, a-a-aren't we?" Freya's voice trembled slightly. "A-a-are you sure we're safe out here?"

"Not scared, are you?" Wulf taunted.

"N-no... Just as long as we can get back safely..."

It was a while before the sleek
vessel sailed into view.

"Hurray!" The children
cheered madly.

Jarl Magnusson stood at the prow. He waved his arms and called to them.

"What did he say?" Vik asked.

"Don't know," said Wulf. "I couldn't hear him properly."

"Never mind," said Vik, as he carried on cheering. "Go, *Dragon*, go!"

Longships

Longships are sleek and deadly warships. They can sail across raging, stormy oceans, and glide up shallow rivers.

Vikings spend their summers sailing on Longships to raid distant villages and steal all their food and treasure.

The children strained to see the last of the *Dragon* as she sailed over the grey horizon and out into the big, wide ocean.

When they turned to go home, the three children had the shock of their lives. They had waited so long for the Dragon to sail past, they hadn't noticed that the tide had turned and the sea level had begun to rise.

Some of the little islands were already underwater!

"Quick! Let's go!" said Vik, leaping across the gap that swirled with foam and rushing water. "We can make it back to shore if we hurry."

It was quite a stretch to the next island. Vik could just see the gravelly rocks under the lapping waves.

"It's not *too* deep," Vik called. "We can wade across if we hold hands and stick together."

Just then, Flek barked.
Freya screamed and
pointed. A long black
fin cut through the
water nearby.

"Orca!" Wulf hissed.

More fins broke
the surface.

Something huge and dark rose out of the water and rolled past the tiny island. A cruel eye watched them and a vicious mouth opened, showing needle-sharp teeth.

They were surrounded by orca – the fierce killer whales.
They were trapped!

"I knew it wasn't safe!"
Freya screamed.

"I don't think they eat people," said Vik, trying to stay calm.

"Well, I don't want to be the first to find out if you're wrong!" said Freya.

"What are we going to do?"
It was Wulf's turn to sound scared.

Vik looked all around for a way out.
Could they get to the shore? Would
the orca eat them alive?

Their best chance was to get back to the island from where they had watched the   sail. It was the largest island with the highest land. Maybe they could survive there until the tide went out again?

Vik made up his mind. They needed to stay alive. They could worry about getting off the island later. "Follow me!" He ordered. "We need to get above the tide."

The children huddled together with
Fleck. The tide crept higher and
higher up the side of the rocky island.
Every few minutes a large wave
lapped the rocks and sprayed them
with foam

"We're lucky it's not windy," Wulf said. "Then the waves would be much higher."

"I wish those horrid orca would go away," Freya whined. Her voice sounded weak and tired.

The orca had all the time in the world. Maybe they were waiting for the children to grow tired and slip into the water!

Could things get any worse?

"What is that?" Vic stared at a huge, dark shape that was rolling towards them from the ocean. It was so large it blackened the sky. Vik remembered how the god, Thor, had battled with Jormungand, the World Serpent.

"Jormungand!" Vik closed his eyes. The monster of the deep was coming to finish them off!"

Thor and Jormungand

Jormungand is the son of
the god Loki. He is so big
that he can wrap his body
around the earth and grasp
his own tail in his mouth.

Legend tells us that, at the
end of the world, Thor will
kill the beast, but not before
Jormungand poisons Thor with
his terrifying teeth.

The wall of darkness
rolled over them like
a cold, wet blanket.
A strange, ghostly,
rhythmic sound echoed
through the foggy mist.
Vik listened hard.

"Jormungand!" He whispered again. "It's coming to get us!"

"I want my dad!" Freya whimpered.

The sound came closer and closer. Fleck barked at the invisible monster.

Suddenly, out of the gloom, a serpent's head towered above them.

The children screamed, and the sound stopped. A familiar voice called through the gloom. "Who's there?"

"I-i-it's me! Vik Harraldson!" Vik yelled.

The Serpent edged closer.

Vik opened his eyes.

It wasn't a serpent…

It was a dragon.

In fact it was *The Dragon*!

Jarl Magnusson's huge face appeared through the mist. "Vik!" He growled. "I told you children to get back to the shore!"

Vik, Freya and Wulf scrambled on board the *Dragon*.

Jarl Magnusson's face softened into a smile. "It's lucky for us that you got stuck out here," he explained. "We were lost in the fog and would've crashed into the rocks, if we hadn't heard Fleck barking. You may well have saved the *Dragon*."

Flek wagged his tail. He knew that he'd done well.

The men began rowing again and the *Dragon* cut through the silent water. Freya told her father all about the orca and the rising tide.

"Well, that's one way to get a ride on a Longship," he laughed when she had finished.

He turned to the boys.
"You two have certainly
learned something
about the dangerous
ways of the ocean
today."

"Yes, sir." The boys hung their heads. They expected Jarl Magnusson to tell them off for getting into such a mess.

He smiled. "Perhaps it's time to let one of you take a longer trip on the *Dragon*."

The two boys eyed each other and smiled secretly to themselves.

Finally each had a chance to sail properly on a Longship. But which one would it be?

"I'm the strongest!" Wulf said, smirking.

Jarl Magnusson's eyes twinkled. "Let's wait until next summer, then we'll see!"

Vik said nothing. He stood
at the prow of the *Dragon*
and felt her racing across the
waves. A competition had begun
between him and Wulf. Vik
was determined to show Jarl
Magnusson that he would be a
worthy winner!

If you enjoyed this book,
then learn to draw Vik and Flek.
and hundreds of other things too .
with Shoo Rayner's famous,
award-winning YouTube videos.

Find out more about Vik
and all Shoo's other books
and get masks and colour-in sheets
at www.shoorayner.com

9 781908 944337